EMERALD AND SHADOW

LILLIANA ROSE

To save her kingdom, she'll bargain with a dragon.

To save his soul, he'll embrace the fae.

CHAPTER 1

M ai

Around me, the unnatural stillness of the forest pressed in, the silence is broken only by the rasping breaths of my warriors.

Ash rained down, coating my skin in a fine gray dust, and the acrid stench of ozone and burned flesh clawed at my throat, a sickening counterpoint to the cloying sweetness of decay. Smoke, gritty and thick, stung my eyes, blurring the edges of the ravaged clearing. It was all a lingering reminder of the fire spell that had barely held back the tide of Gloom.

The Gloomlings had retreated, slithering back

into the oppressive shadows that clung to the edges of the clearing, but the air itself felt heavy and suffocating, a constant reminder of their presence, a parasitic chill that seemed to leech the very warmth from the sun.

My warriors, their faces smudged with soot and exhaustion, mirrored my own grim reflection. Magic, usually a vibrant pulse beneath our skin, now felt like a dying ember. We hadn't lost this battle. Not yet. But the victory was a phantom, a fleeting respite in a war that was slowly consuming us.

My fingers, numb with cold, traced the jagged edge of a scorched tree trunk. The wood crumbled, dry and lifeless.

"Commander..." Theron's deep rumble broke the silence beside me. He shifted uneasily, avoiding my gaze. "Orders?" His normally vibrant blue eyes were dull, clouded with a weariness that mirrored my own.

The first wave of Gloom, orchestrated by Erebus and the Nightshade... whispers of forbidden rituals, of shadows embraced...

"How many?" The words were a choked whisper, barely audible above the painful groans of the wounded.

"Twelve, Commander." Theron's tone was flat,

devoid of emotion. He, too, carried the weight of this war.

Twelve. *Twelve.* The number echoed in my mind, each repetition a hammer blow against my resolve. Twelve families shattered. My fingers tightened on the scorched bark, grounding me against the rising tide of despair.

My gaze swept over the clearing, each fallen Dark Fae a fresh stab of grief. Their wings, once vibrant and iridescent, lay broken and tattered. The Gloomlings left no physical wounds, only this. Emptiness. Husks. Like my mother.

The memory of her vacant eyes, the chilling absence of her vibrant spirit.

"See to the fallen," I choked out, the words catching in my throat. "Take them back to the castle." My own golden wings, usually a source of pride, felt heavy, useless.

I am the commander. The next queen.

The crown felt heavy, a leaden weight pressing down on me, crushing me beneath the weight of responsibility. How many more lives would be lost before I, too, became another empty husk, a victim of Erebus' insatiable ambition? His twisted whispers of a new Aethel, fueled by shadow and decay, promised power, but at what cost?

A commotion erupted at the edge of the clearing.

Two warriors dragged a struggling figure toward me, his dark robes torn, his face contorted in fear. "Commander," one of the warriors called out. "We found this one hiding. He bears the mark of the Nightshade."

A traitor.

A flicker of hope ignited within me. Perhaps this captive held the key to ending the Gloom, to stopping Erebus. I straightened, my wings settling, the weight of command returning. "Bring him closer," I ordered, my voice regaining its steel. "Let's see what secrets he holds."

The captive, a wiry Dark Fae with the Nightshade's mark—a stylized nightshade flower tattooed on his wrist—trembled before me, his eyes darting nervously between the grim-faced warriors flanking him and me. The air around him thrummed with a palpable fear, tinged with the scent of decaying vegetation, a ghostly echo of the Gloom.

"Speak." The single word, sharp and cold, echoed in the sudden stillness, a demand that hung heavy in the air.

"I'll tell you nothing, fae bitch! The Nightshade will prevail!"

A ribbon of emerald fire sparked from my fingertips and coiled around his throat, cutting off his defiant words. This was my only chance.

Theron stepped forward, his hand hovering over his sword. "The commander asked you a question," he growled out.

The captive's eyes bulged, and I loosened the magical grip slightly, just enough for him to gasp out a desperate plea. "Erebus… attacks again."

"When?"

"Three days… the final assault… five armies strong…"

Five armies?

My breath hitched. How? He'd tripled his forces. Impossible. Icy dread spread through my veins. We were outnumbered, outmatched. We needed a miracle.

"Anything else?"

He shook his head frantically.

I tightened the emerald fire once again, his choking sound spurring me on for what awaited me. Theron's sword flashed, and the traitor's sounds were swallowed by the forest.

Three days.

A miracle.

Or Aethel was lost.

And now… now I had to face my father. The king. Who still believed in the power of antiquated rituals and empty pronouncements, oblivious to the true threat that loomed over our kingdom. My wings snapped open, the gilded edges catching the last rays of the setting sun, the light tinged with the sickly green of the retreating Gloom.

This battle might be over, but the war was far from won.

CHAPTER 2

M ai

A chill, deeper than the Gloom that plagued my kingdom, settled over my wings as I touched down on the castle's landing platform. Nightspire, our ancestral castle, with its pristine walls and hushed whispers, felt a world away from the ravaged battle-field, away from the reality of the war that was about to consume us all.

Three days.

The constant thought echoed the frantic beating of her heart. Three days until Erebus unleashed his final assault. I hadn't even paused to clean the grime from my armor, the dust a physical manifestation of the weight I carried.

I burst into the throne room, my unannounced arrival causing the assembled courtiers to gasp and murmur. My father, King Eldrin, sat on his throne, his shoulders slumped, his usually vibrant silver hair dull and lifeless. He looked every bit his age, the weight of the crown a visible burden.

"Mai," he said, his voice weary. "Did you defeat those bastards?"

"We held them off..." I breathed deep, the emotion felt in my bones, "... but at a cost."

"A cost?" He frowned, his brow furrowing. "How many?"

"Twelve, My King."

A flicker of grief crossed his face, quickly replaced by a mask of stoic resolve. "A tragic loss," he murmured, his gaze distant. "But we will honor their sacrifice. We will rally our forces, strengthen our resolve. The truth and light of our ancient rituals will prevail over the dark magic of the Nightshade."

My jaw tightened. My father's naïve faith in outdated rituals infuriated me. The stench of smoke and burned earth still clung to me, a stark reminder of the reality he refused to acknowledge. "Father," I said, my voice rising above the hushed whispers of the court. "We cannot simply rally. Erebus has *five* armies. We're outnumbered, outmatched. He plans a final assault in *three* days. We won't survive."

"You of little faith." His response echoed strangely in the vast throne room. It lacked the resonance of command, the strength I craved in a leader. "Of course, we will survive. And we will do better than that. We *will* win." He puffed out his chest, a pathetic attempt to project an authority he didn't possess. His eyes, however, darted nervously around the room, betraying his false bravado.

"Father," I pleaded. "We barely have one army now. The Gloomlings have taken our power. They feed on our magic, Father, leaving us weak, vulnerable."

"I am your king!" he shouted, his outburst more petulant than powerful.

I bowed my head, the weight of the predestined crown, the one I should be wearing, pressed down on me. I forced myself to show respect to my king, my father, the man who was about to lead them all to our deaths. Shame washed over me as I felt the weight of the court's gazes, their silent pleas for me to act, to challenge him, to take control. *Could I usurp my own father?* Even with the Gloom closing in, the thought felt like a betrayal.

He grumbled, a low, guttural sound, then cleared his throat, attempting to regain a semblance of composure. He sat up straighter, pointing a trembling finger at me. "We *will* win."

"Sire, we will." I met his gaze, my emerald eyes blazing with a determination he couldn't comprehend. *We will win,* I vowed silently because I would find a way.

"But we can't do it alone." I spoke each word carefully as if they were a stone in the foundation of our kingdom.

"We can. This is our fight, no one else's." He retreated into the familiar comfort of isolationism, his gaze fixed on some distant point beyond the throne room walls.

"But the Nightshade… if they…" I swallowed, the words catching in my throat. "With them in power, the death, the pain they will inflict on the fae… and then the other realms… we can't be complacent. We need a plan."

"I have a plan. To fight. And you are the commander. Any failure today falls on your shoulders."

His words were barbed arrows, piercing my armor, striking at the heart of my loyalty. *It is my fault,* I thought bitterly, *for letting you believe we could win this war without help.*

"The Gloomlings have taken our power, weakened us." I kept my tone even, desperately trying to reason with him.

"Then get stronger!" His words echoed the hollowness of his authority.

I didn't suppress the sigh this time. It escaped my lips, a ragged breath of frustration that echoed in the sudden silence of the throne room. The weight of the court's gazes pressed down on me, their silent pleas for action a tangible force. I met their eyes, a spark of defiance igniting in my own.

He won't act, I realized, a chilling certainty settling in my heart.

But I will.

"Very well, Father," I said, deceptively calm. "I will rally the troops. And I will also seek the aid we so desperately need."

My wings snapped open, a silent challenge to his authority, and I strode toward the exit, ignoring his sputtering protests, the whispers of the courtiers following me like a phantom army. I had no time for his denial, his outdated rituals. Aethel's fate rested on my shoulders, and I would not fail.

"No."

I turned at his rebuttal and watched as he dismissed my plea with a wave of his hand as if swatting away a bothersome insect.

"My King, I would only be gone a day. Just to secure the aid we desperately need."

"No. You need to rally the army, prepare for the next attack."

"Theron can do that. My journey would be worth the risk if I returned with reinforcements."

"No one will support us." His certainty bordered on delusion.

"They will." I clung to that hope, fragile as it was. But who? Who could I turn to? The Dark Fae had more enemies than allies.

"I won't be long. You'll see." I straightened my back, my wings shifting restlessly behind me.

I would not beg.

Not even with my father.

CHAPTER 3

Mai

Inside my chambers, I paused, my gaze drawn to the familiar paintings above the fireplace. One depicted the vibrant Earth Realm, a world of life and color I'd only ever glimpsed in these images. Beside it, dragons soared through a stormy sky, their scales shimmering, their breath fire against the clouds.

Dragons.

Myth.

Lost.

A pang of longing, sharp and bittersweet, pierced my heart.

Dragon shifters.

The whispered rumors, the ancient prophecies…

They existed.

Hidden amongst the humans in the Earth Realm. A spark of hope ignited within me, a fire in the encroaching Gloom. If anyone could help me save Aethel, it would be them. My jaw set, my wings settling into a determined stillness.

I would find them.

I had to.

Aethel's fate, and my own, depended on it.

The portal spat me out onto the rain-slicked streets of Hobart, the Human Realm, a jarring assault of unfamiliar scents and sounds. My lungs burned with the acrid stench of exhaust fumes, a stark contrast to the crisp air of Aethel. And beneath that…

I swallowed hard against the rising bile in my throat. The Gloom. The realization sent a shiver of cold dread down my spine. Impossible. Yet, the scent, faint but unmistakable, clung to the air, a ghostly whisper in the alien night.

Had I brought it with me? Had the Gloom, that insidious, life-draining force, somehow latched onto me, followed me across realms, its tendrils already reaching, seeking to consume me even here in the Human Realm?

I couldn't understand why the dragon shifters had retreated here, seeking refuge in this world, hiding amongst the oblivious humans. Tasmania, remote, isolated, a place where the whispers of magic still clung to the land, a place where dragons might yet find solace.

My glamour, woven from moonlight and shadow, masked my true form, presenting me as a human woman, my golden wings and pointed ears concealed beneath the illusion. I blended in with the late-night crowd, and my Dark Fae senses were alert for any hint of dragon magic, which led me to a dimly lit pub, the raucous laughter and the smell of stale beer spilling out onto the street.

The air in the pub crackled with hidden energy, a subtle thrumming beneath the surface of raucous laughter and clinking glasses. I found them. Not the majestic, fire-breathing beasts of legend. Men and women gathered around worn wooden tables, their dragon forms cloaked beneath layers of human illusion.

Doubt pricked at me. Were these truly the creatures who held the fate of Aethel in their claws? Could these seemingly ordinary humans, so at ease in this mundane world, possibly understand the desperation clawing at my soul? *A dragon's fire could burn through the Gloomlings before we were drained,* I reminded myself, clinging to that sliver of hope.

I had no other choice.

I approached the Stormwing leader, a man named Gavril. His grizzled features and piercing gaze held the only hint of his true nature. His eyes, a startling shade of molten gold, shimmered with an unsettling reptilian gleam. The scent of him, faint but unmistakable—the primal musk of dragon—sent a shiver of anticipation down my spine.

"I am Mai Nightbloom of Aethel," I announced, my voice echoing with the authority of my lineage, an authority I prayed my glamour couldn't fully conceal. "I request your help."

Gavril leaned back, a slow, predatory smile spreading across his face. "Look at this," he said, amusement lighting his hard features. "A fae princess begging at our table." A ripple of laughter spread through the group, their sneers like daggers aimed at my already fragile confidence.

"I wouldn't come to you if I had any other choice," I retorted, tight with suppressed fury.

"Is that so, Princess?" Gavril's smile widened, revealing a flash of sharp teeth. "I hear whispers of troubled times in Aethel. Tell me, what brings a royal such as yourself to this… unrefined establishment?"

"The Nightshade, led by my Uncle Erebus, is destroying my kingdom," I said, forcing myself to sound confident despite the tremor of fear that ran through me. "They wield the Gloom, a power that drains the life from the land. We are losing. We need your help… your fire."

His smile vanished, replaced by a mask of cold indifference. "The Gloom? A fool's errand to fight it. Accept your fate, Princess. Erebus will make a… suitable king. Perhaps even a husband for a desperate princess."

Fury, hot and sharp, threatened to overwhelm me. "Suitable? He murdered my mother! He will destroy Aethel, and then he will not stop! He craves power, dominion over all the realms…"

Gavril shrugged, his indifference a physical blow. "Let him try." He scoffed, taking another swig of his beer. "We'll be waiting. This isn't our fight, Princess. Now run along before they kill your father. It would be… convenient for you to be by his side when he falls, wouldn't it?"

"You're the leader of the clan," I argued, the words raw with desperation, each syllable a plea, a demand. My throat tightened, the unspoken fear of Aethel's fate, of my own impending doom, choking me. "This is your duty. You cannot abandon us to the Gloom." My hand instinctively went to the faint scars on my arm, a visceral reminder of a Gloomling attack, the chilling touch, the draining sensation, the lingering weakness that had plagued me for weeks.

A dragon's fire could burn through them, I reminded myself. A desperate flicker of hope in the encroaching darkness. Incinerate them before they even have a chance to drain our magic. I had to get them to help. There was no other choice.

Gavril's laughter, harsh and grating, like the scraping of steel against stone, was a physical blow. "Duty?" He scoffed again, the word a mockery on his lips. He took another long swig of his beer, the golden liquid a grotesque parody of the dragon fire I so desperately craved. "My only duty is to my clan, to our survival. And that means staying far, far away from the suicidal affairs of the Dark Fae."

He slammed his beer mug down on the table, the sound echoing in the sudden silence, a final punctuation mark on his dismissal. "Now leave, little princess, before I decide to make an example of you." His golden eyes, predatory as a hawk's, fixed on me, promised a swift and merciless end should I draw another breath. "I assure you," he added, his voice low, dangerous, a cruel smile twisting his lips. "A dragon's fire is not always… merciful."

Gavril's laughter echoed in my ears, a cruel mockery of my desperation. The dismissal was absolute. The chilling promise of what he could unleash hung in the air, thick and suffocating, a visceral reminder of the power I couldn't control, the power I so desperately needed.

No help here. Aethel, my people, my father… all lost.

The image of Erebus, leering and triumphant, flashed through my mind. He wouldn't just take the throne. He would revel in our suffering, turning Aethel into a desolate wasteland, a monument to his twisted ambition. And me? I shuddered, unwilling to imagine my fate at his hands.

I fled the pub, the raucous laughter pursuing me like a pack of hounds. The cool night air was thick with the unfamiliar scents of the Human Realm, each one jarring with its sharpness on my fae senses. The brightly lit storefronts, the garish advertisements, and the numerous conversations from energetic humans milling in the street, ready to party, were so loud and brash. So utterly alien. Each sight, each sound, was a painful reminder of the delicate beauty of Aethel, the whispering forests, the shimmering rivers, the soft glow of the moonwillow blossoms all fading, dying, under the suffocating grasp of the Gloom.

As despair threatened to consume me, a spark of emerald green, vibrant and insistent, cut through the despair of my thoughts. It pulsed with an energy that resonated deep within my soul, a vibrant spark in the encroaching darkness. As I followed its pull, it intensified, drawing me down a narrow, cobbled street, the gaslights casting long, dancing shadows that seemed to twist and writhe with a life of their own. The air around me crackled, charged with an unfamiliar magic. A subtle scent, like woodsmoke and old parchment, drifted on the breeze, growing stronger with each step.

At the end of the street, nestled between a bustling tavern and a silent apothecary, stood a small, unassuming bookstore. The emerald spark pulsed brighter, warmer as I approached, my fingers tingling in response. The sign above the door, barely visible in the fading light, seemed to shimmer and shift before my eyes. The Inkwell.

A strange sense of anticipation, a premonition of something both wondrous and dangerous, settled over me. I hesitated, my hand hovering over the doorknob before pushing open the door, a small bell tinkling in the stillness.

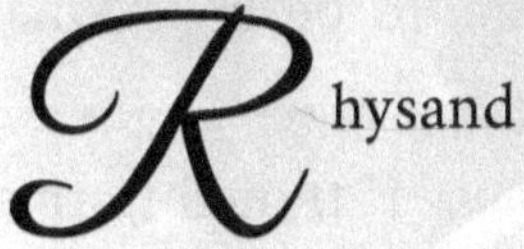hysand

My fingers traced the worn leather of the *Drakon's Codex*, the mythical text a tangible weight in my hands. It was the real *Codex*, the legendary grimoire rumored to hold the key to… well, everything. A reminder of the power I had lost, the power I craved to reclaim. I sighed, the familiar ache of disappointment settling in my chest. Perhaps, hidden within these forged pages there might be a clue, a hint, a whisper of the true *Codex's* location.

The bell above the door chimed, drawing me back to the present. I slipped the forgery into the drawer beneath my desk, its presence a secret shame, a persistent reminder of my failure. A couple, giddy with drink, stumbled out, their laughter echoing in the night. I emerged from behind my desk, my gaze lingering on the rosewood bookshelf in the far corner, my sanctuary within a sanctuary, where the real magic resided, hidden from human eyes.

Inside, amongst the genuine grimoires and ancient texts, lay the true objects of my desire, not just the *Drakon's Codex*, but the power it represented, the power to reclaim my heritage, to perhaps, one day, return to the Stormwing clan.

At least books can't betray you, I thought, the familiar mantra a shield against the ever-present ache of loneliness.

I picked up a slim, leather-bound volume, *The Grimoire of Minor Conjurations*. The minor spells were a pale echo of my dragon magic, but they were something. A connection, however tenuous, to the life I had lost, the life I had sacrificed for Elara. The memory of her laughter, sharp and bittersweet, pierced through my carefully constructed defenses.

I walked to the rosewood shelves and inhaled the familiar scent of aged parchment and leather-bound magic. As I slid the grimoire into place, a faint emerald light flickered from behind surrounding books. It pulsed with an unfamiliar energy, a subtle hum that vibrated against my skin.

Odd. I stood and reached for the closest book, and my hand brushed against another, smaller, warmer hand.

That's when I saw her, standing there, bathed in the emerald glow, her eyes, the same mesmerizing shade, fixed on mine. A spark of energy, not just magical, but something more, leaped between us.

I recoiled, with a low growl rumbling in my chest. "Sorry," I muttered, turning to face the intruder.

And then I forgot how to breathe.

Her eyes, the color of emeralds, met mine, and a jolt, like a surge of raw magic, shot through me. She was breathtaking. Her beauty was otherworldly, yet there was a strength, a fierceness in her gaze that resonated deep within my soul. I smiled, a genuine smile, and she smiled back, a slow curve of her lips that sent a wave of heat through me.

What was a human doing so close to the special edition books?

"Can I help you?" I asked in a husky whisper. "These books are… well, not for everyone."

"I'm not everyone," she replied, her voice like velvet.

Rhysand, I chided myself. *Get a grip.* But my gaze

was locked on hers. "I'm Rhysand," I managed. "This is my store. Are you looking for something in particular?"

"Yes," she said, her emerald eyes fixed on mine. "A book. One to banish monsters."

My heart skipped a beat. Banish monsters… *The Drakon's Codex?* Could it be? No. Just a coincidence. A human wouldn't be looking for that.

She reached into the shelves, her fingers brushing against the book that had glowed green. "It's not that one," she said, her voice like velvet, pulling out a different volume, its spine unmarked.

We both reached for it, our fingers brushing. A spark, stronger this time, more insistent, a jolt of emerald fire, passed between us. My heart pounded against my ribs, a frantic drumbeat against the sudden, inexplicable pull I felt toward her, a pull that was more than just physical, a resonance of magic, of something… *familiar.*

I looked at her, my gaze drawn to the emerald fire flickering in her eyes, a mirror of the spark that had led her to me, to this bookstore, to this moment. She met my gaze, her eyes shimmering, a silent question, an unspoken invitation, in their depths.

No way is she human…

The thought echoed as my gaze traced the curve of her neck, the line of her jaw. I noticed a faint shimmer, a ripple in the air, where her glamour faltered, her desire, a wildfire mirroring my own, burning through the illusion.

For a fleeting second, I saw them—the tips of her wings, delicate and iridescent, the color of moonlight on emeralds, tucked carefully against her back. *Fae.*

We stood, our bodies almost touching, the air between us crackling with an energy I hadn't felt in decades, a forgotten language of desire and longing, of a connection that transcended words, that defied explanation. I wanted to touch her again, to feel the spark ignite between us, to lose myself in the emerald fire of her gaze, to explore the magic that shimmered beneath her skin, the power that pulsed in her veins. The realization, a thrilling and terrifying jolt, went down my spine. Fae.

I want her anyway.

And then, I did something I hadn't done in years.

I leaned forward and kissed her.

Mai

The world tilted, the scent of old paper and woodsmoke filling my senses, grounding me in the present, in the warmth of Rhysand's lips on mine. The cool emerald flicker had led me here, but a searing, white-hot flame ignited between us, burning away the chill of the Gloom, the weight of my responsibilities, the fear that had been my constant companion for so long.

I gasped, my hands instinctively rising to his chest, the solid warmth of his body a stark contrast to the chilling emptiness that haunted my dreams, the emptiness that was slowly consuming my kingdom.

I should have pulled away.

I knew I should have.

My mission, my dying Aethel, my role as commander was a lead weight. All of it screamed at me to stop, to remember why I was here.

But I couldn't.

It was as if the emerald magic, the very force that had guided me, now flowed between us, a current of raw energy, urging me closer, whispering promises of forgotten pleasures, of a warmth I hadn't realized I craved.

His hands tangled in my hair, his touch sending shivers down my spine, igniting a fire that spread through my veins, melting away the ice that had encased my heart for centuries. The kiss deepened, a desperate, hungry exploration that stole the breath from my lungs, a delicious ache that resonated deep within my soul.

I moaned, the sound muffled against his lips, a sound I hadn't realized I was capable of making, one of pure, unadulterated pleasure.

I hadn't felt this alive in centuries. The endless war against the Gloom, the ever-present ache of my mother's loss had all taken its toll, extinguishing the fire within me, leaving me cold, empty, a hollow shell.

His touch, his taste, the heat of him against me was rekindling that flame, awakening a part of me I had long since buried, a part of me I'd believed lost forever.

A low growl, a primal rumble deep within him, vibrated against my skin, a sound that resonated with something ancient, something... *not human.*

He wasn't just a man.

The realization hit me with the force of a physical blow, the truth of it echoing with the spark of magic that had led me to him, to this moment.

He was a dragon shifter. A potential savior. A spark in the suffocating darkness, a promise of warmth and light in my shadowed world.

He was forbidden.

Dangerous.

Everything I shouldn't crave.

Especially a dragon.

Our kinds were ancient enemies, our histories intertwined in a tapestry of blood and betrayal. But at that moment, pressed against him, his lips crushing mine, his hands igniting my skin, his magic intertwining with my own in a dance of emerald and shadow, none of that mattered.

The world outside the bookstore, the dying kingdom, the looming threat of Erebus... all of it faded, lost in the intoxicating heat of the moment, in the raw, visceral need that pulsed between us, a need that transcended ancient rivalries, that whispered of a connection deeper than blood, deeper than magic, a connection that felt like... *destiny.*

His hands, hot and demanding, moved down my back, his touch sending shivers of anticipation through me. He lingered over the curve of my ass, his fingers squeezing, possessing, branding me as his. A gasp escaped my lips as a wave of heat, raw and intense, radiated through me. I couldn't help but arch into him, my body yearning for closer contact, the world outside the bookstore fading into a hazy, insignificant blur. *This is wrong,* a thought whispered in the back of my mind. *Dangerous.* But the inner voice was weak, drowned out by the rising tide of desire, the intoxicating scent of his skin, the feel of his hard body pressed against mine.

He groaned, a low rumble in his chest that vibrated against my skin, his body molding against mine, the heat of him searing through the flimsy fabric of my borrowed human clothes.

He walked me back, the hard edge of his bookshelf digging into my back, a welcome anchor in the swirling desire consuming me. His large frame caged me, pressing into me and sending books to the floor, their pages rustling like whispers of encouragement, forgotten stories momentarily eclipsed by the story we were writing with our bodies, our breaths, our intertwined souls. His hands, strong and sure, explored the curves of my body beneath the borrowed fabric, his touch sending waves of pleasure radiating through me. The glamour, still clinging to me like a second skin, felt like a cage, a barrier between us, a veil I desperately wanted to shed.

His lips trailed fire down my neck, his breath a brand against my skin. Each kiss, a possessive mark, a claim staked upon my soul. *His.* The word echoed in my mind, a forbidden thrill, a dangerous surrender. A hunger, sharp as a dragon's claw, awakened within me, a reflection of the desire burning in his eyes.

My fingers dug into his shoulders, the muscles taut beneath my fingertips, anchoring me to the present, to the intoxicating reality of his touch. I arched my back, my body yearning for closer contact. The world outside the bookstore, the weight of my crown, the looming threat of Erebus... all of it was fading, dissolving into the background as the raw, visceral need that pulsed between us threatened to consume me entirely.

This is madness. The thought whispered in the back of my mind.

But the madness felt exquisite.

I wanted him with a fierceness that surprised even me, a need that transcended the political machinations of my world, the impending doom of my kingdom. It was all lost in the haze of desire, replaced by the need that pulsed between us.

Right then, there was only Rhysand, his touch, his taste, his scent, a heady mix of woodsmoke, old paper, and something uniquely intoxicatingly him. And me, surrendering to a desire I had no right to feel, a desire that threatened to consume me, body and soul, a desire that felt like coming home.

His mouth, hot and insistent, trailed a heated path along my collarbone, his breath a whisper of promise against my skin. He paused at the neckline of my T-shirt, his teeth grazing the thin fabric. My fingers tangled in his hair, urging him closer. I didn't want him to stop. Not now. Not ever. With a gasp, I reached down, grabbed the hem of my top, and pulled it over my head, the soft cotton clinging momentarily to my skin before falling away, leaving me bare beneath his hungry gaze.

A low growl, a sound of pure, unadulterated desire, rumbled in his chest, and his lips continued their descent, his touch sending waves of heat radiating through me. His hand, firm and gentle, cupped my breast before his fingers deftly unclasped my bra, pushing the lacy fabric aside as his mouth closed over my nipple, his tongue swirling, teasing, drawing a moan from deep within me. His other hand slid down my back, his fingers pressing into my skin, anchoring me to the present, to the exquisite pleasure of his touch.

A need to feel his skin against mine, to erase the last vestiges of separation between us, surged through me. I reached for his shirt, my fingers fumbling with the buttons, my impatience growing with each one. With a growl, I tugged, ripping the buttons free, sending them scattering across the bookstore, pinging off the spines of unsuspecting volumes.

A giggle, breathless and unexpected, escaped my lips, a release of the tension that had coiled tight within me for so long. He smiled, a slow, seductive curve of his lips that sent a shiver down my spine as he shrugged the shirt off his shoulders. It fell away to reveal the sculpted planes of his chest, the smooth, tanned skin, and the muscles rippling beneath the surface.

My breath hitched. He was beautiful. Powerful.

And the thought of him in his dragon form, scales shimmering, wings unfurled, fire blazing...

the image sent a wave of heat through me, a longing so intense it ached. He would be magnificent.

My fingers traced the contours of his chest, the skin smooth and warm beneath my touch. Unable to resist, I leaned in, my lips brushing against his, the taste of him familiar, intoxicating.

He groaned, a low rumble in his chest, and his hands found the waistband of my pants, his fingers deftly unbuttoning them. There was no denying whatever this was building between us.

I wanted him.

Here.

Now.

Surrounded by the silent whispers of forgotten stories and their scent, a strange, intoxicating mix of the mundane and the magical.

He pushed my pants down my hips, his gaze never leaving mine, a silent question, a plea for permission, burning in his amber eyes. I nodded, my own desire a mirror of his, a wildfire ignited by his touch. Beneath the surface, a deeper current flowed —a need not just for physical pleasure but for connection, for solace, for a moment of respite from the suffocating darkness of my world.

He gripped my hips and moved me, urging me backward until my legs met the edge of his desk. Then, as if I weighed nothing, he lifted me and set me on the old wood surface with a soft thud and a rustle of aged paper.

Rhysand followed, his body crushing mine, his warmth a brand against my skin. A welcome anchor in the swirling desire that filled me. And as his lips found mine once more, a searing, white-hot flame igniting between us, I wasn't just lost in the pleasure but in the feeling—the raw vulnerability, the shared intimacy, the unspoken promise of a connection that transcended the physical.

For the first time since my mother's death, since the encroaching darkness of the Gloom had begun to consume my world, I felt safe. Protected. As I wrapped my arms around him, my fingers digging into his back, I knew, with a certainty that defied logic, that I wasn't lost.

I was… home.

His fingers, warm and sure, traced a path of fire down my side, lingering over the faded scars that marked my ribs, a silent testament to battles fought and won, his touch a gentle caress against the reminders of my past. Then he dipped lower, gliding over the curve of my hip, tracing the delicate line of my thigh before venturing into the heat between my legs. A gasp, sharp and involuntary, escaped my lips without my permission as his touch, now intimate, possessive, ignited a fire deep within me. I arched my back, my hips rising to meet his hand, my body thrumming with a need so intense it bordered on pain.

I was ready for him.

I needed him.

Now.

My hands, impatient, fumbled with the button and zipper of his jeans, the denim a frustrating barrier between us. I wanted him naked, skin against skin, his heat branding me, claiming me. He chuckled, a low rumble in his chest, and helped to shed the last of his clothes, his amber eyes burning with a desire. Then, we were flesh against flesh, his hardness pressing into the soft skin of my belly, a delicious ache that sent a wave of heat through me.

My fingers traced the contours of his back, the muscles rippling beneath my touch, then around his hips, where I gripped his length, my fingers tightening around his hardness, drawing a moan from his lips. I moved my hand, slowly at first, then with increasing urgency, savoring the feel of him, the power, the heat.

He groaned, rocking into me, his breath hot against my ear, and then, with a sudden surge of strength, he lifted me. My legs instinctively wrapped around his waist, and I reluctantly let him go, encircling my hands around his neck. He carried me, our bodies pressed together, our lips locked in a desperate, hungry kiss, toward a room.

With each step, his hard length slid against me, working me up until I couldn't help but chase the promise of release. With blinded, unbridled abandon, I ground against him until my vision threatened to turn black. A sense of relief washed through me as my hearing muffled. It wasn't until Rhysand's deep growl reverberated through me that the world around us came crashing back.

"Fucking perfection," he gritted out, lowering me gently to the floor, my knees weak, my body still thrumming with the aftershocks of pleasure.

My breath came in heavy pants, and I watched as he gathered blankets from the nearby couch, arranging them on the floor with a tenderness that belied the intensity of our passion. Then, he kneeled before me, his gaze locked on mine, a silent question in his amber eyes.

I nodded, my body aching for him, and he lowered his head, his lips pressing against the soft skin of my belly, his touch sending a rush of excitement through me. He moved lower, his tongue tracing a path of fire between my thighs, dipping into my wet heat, his touch a charge of pure pleasure. I released a gasp from the connection, not just physical but something deeper. It lit me up from the inside out. I shifted, resting back on my forearms as my fingers tangled in his hair, urging him closer.

Wave after wave of sensation crashed over me, my body shuddering with the force of it.

He looked up, a mischievous grin spreading across his face, his eyes alight with a shared pleasure. I couldn't resist. I sat up, getting on my knees and pushing him gently backward until he lay beneath me.

I straddled him, my core aligning with his hardness, the anticipation almost unbearable. With a low moan, I rocked my hips forward, his hands gripping my hips. The movement lined his head up with where I needed him most. I couldn't stop myself even if I wanted to. I sank myself back, my muscles contracting around him, welcoming him home. His groan of pleasure matched my own, and the world narrowed, sharpened, focusing on the exquisite friction, the heightened pleasure of our joined bodies.

I moved slowly at first, savoring each sensation, then faster, harder, my breath coming in ragged gasps, my body burning with a need that demanded another release. And then, it hit me, a tsunami of pure bliss that rippled through me, my muscles clenching around him as he shuddered beneath me, his release a series of hard, insistent pulses. I collapsed onto him, my body still trembling, our breaths mingling, our hearts beating a frantic rhythm against each other, the world outside the bookstore forgotten in the aftermath of our shared pleasure.

But as I lay there, wrapped in his arms, the scent of his skin, of our lovemaking, filling my senses, a chilling thought pierced through the haze of satisfaction.

What have I done?

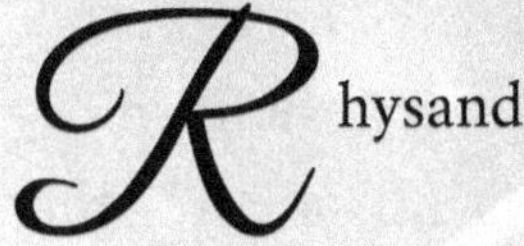 hysand

A phantom scent of jasmine and woodsmoke, a cruel reminder of last night's passion, clung to the air, mocking my solitude. I reached over, expecting the familiar warmth of her body beside me, but found only the cool blankets. Sitting up, the covers tangled around my waist, my gaze tracing the contours of the rumpled material, the indentation where her body had lain.

We'd made love there, amongst the scattered cushions, our passion, a chaotic symphony against the backdrop of silent stories. I could still feel the ghost of her touch, the echo of our shared pleasure in the stillness of the morning.

And beneath the surface, a deeper current flowed. Fear. I hadn't allowed myself to be this vulnerable, this connected, since Elara. Since I'd fallen in love with a human and been outcast from my clan, the shame of that rejection, the searing pain of exile, a brand on my soul.

Don't be a fool, Rhysand, I chided myself, my heart a painful knot in my chest.

She's fae. You're a broken dragon. It will never work.

But even as I told myself those lies, the memory of her emerald eyes, blazing with a fire that mirrored my own, the way her magic had intertwined with mine, a dance of emerald and shadow, the feel of her skin beneath my fingertips, smooth as moonlight, warm as dragon fire… it all whispered a different story. A story of hope, connection, one I desperately wanted to believe, something that both terrified and exhilarated me.

Her presence, not just a physical sensation, was a subtle hum of magic that resonated with the dormant power within me, a pull that transcended the physical realm, a siren's call in the quiet dawn.

I found her by the rosewood bookshelf, its glass door ajar, a silent invitation into the world of magic I had kept hidden for so long. Her slender fingers traced the spine of *Demonology: A Practitioner's Guide.* *She pulled it from the shelf, opened the book, and began reading.*

She was now dressed in black, clearly manifested with fae magic—tight leather pants and a sleeveless top that accentuated her long legs and the elegant line of her neck. Her raven hair, unbound, cascaded down her back like a silken waterfall. Even in the dim light of the bookstore, she was breathtaking. And utterly forbidden. My heart ached with a longing so intense it was almost painful, a longing that whispered of a future I couldn't imagine, a future I both craved and feared.

"I would say, why don't you come back to bed," I murmured, my croaky rough with sleep. "But I suppose the ground is a little uncomfortable… still…"

She turned, a slow, seductive smile spreading across her lips. "You're keen."

"You make me keen," I admitted, my voice husky, the fire within me rekindled by her presence, burning brighter, hotter. I reached out, tucking a stray strand of hair behind her ear, my fingers lingering against her skin, savoring the warmth, the softness, the subtle difference that had been there all along, a whisper of magic beneath the surface.

"I know what you are," she said, her emerald eyes

locking with mine, a knowing glint in their depths, a spark of something that looked almost like… *triumph?* She snapped the Demonology book shut, the sound echoing in the sudden tension that filled the air.

"And what am I, then?" I asked, my voice a low murmur, the question a mixture of curiosity and a strange, unsettling premonition.

"What I need." Her voice was low, husky, a seductive purr that sent a shiver down my spine. For a heartbeat, I allowed myself to believe she was talking about the passion we had shared, the fire that had burned so brightly between us.

"Then let's get back to it," I said playfully, a desperate attempt to recapture the easy intimacy we had shared, to banish the sudden unease that had settled between us.

She chuckled, a low, throaty sound that sent a wave of heat through me. "Not that… though I did enjoy it." She stood, her fluid grace, the way she moved, so different from a human, a silent testament to her fae heritage, sending a fresh wave of desire through me.

I want her again. The thought, raw and insistent, warred with the rising tide of uncertainty.

"You're a dragon shifter," she stated, her voice low and serious, the words a simple truth, yet they felt like an accusation. Her gaze, sharp and piercing, seemed to see right through me into the very heart of my carefully guarded secret.

"Not anymore," I admitted, the words a bitter taste in my mouth, a confession of my failure, my weakness. The shame, hot and sharp, twisted in my gut. "I'm… alone. No clan. Broken." I looked away, unable to meet her gaze, the weight of her unspoken judgment, of my own self-disgust, pressing down on me. "And you… you're fae."

"Dark Fae," she corrected, the word hanging in the air between us, a stark reminder of the chasm that separated our worlds, our species.

I hadn't thought it possible, but my situation had just plummeted to new depths. My flesh, my desires… they were my weakness, my curse. They had led me to Elara, to exile, to this…

… this impossible situation.

"You should be repelled by me," I said in a desperate plea for her to leave, to save me from the dangerous pull I felt toward her, to save her from the disappointment I knew I would inevitably cause.

"I wasn't. And neither were you." Her gaze flicked down to my arousal, a playful smile returning to her lips, but it didn't reach her eyes. "And you still aren't."

Heat flooded my cheeks, shame mixing with the

lingering desire. "Well, we could do something about that," I muttered, the words a lighthearted banter.

"Hmm… tempting." She held the Demonology book close, her fingers tracing the embossed cover, then stepped closer, her body brushing against mine, the warmth of her skin igniting a familiar fire in my blood.

My cock pressed against her belly, a hard, insistent reminder of our shared passion, a passion that now felt complicated. She trailed a finger along my collarbone, the touch sending a shiver down my spine, a flicker of pleasure, something that now felt forbidden. I'd been alone for too long. Too long without touch, without connection, without *her*.

"Why don't you change for me?" she whispered, her breath warm against my ear, the words a seductive invitation, a challenge.

"I change for no one," I growled out, the words a lie, a shield against the shame of my inability to shift, a desperate attempt to maintain some semblance of control in a situation that was rapidly spiraling beyond my grasp.

"Please." She nipped at the base of my neck, her teeth grazing my skin, sending a jolt of pure desire through me, a desire that warred with the growing sense of dread, the knowledge that I couldn't give her what she wanted, what she needed.

"I… I can't." The words were a strangled whisper, a confession of my failure. I pushed her away, the force of my rejection surprising us both, a physical manifestation of the emotional chasm that had opened between us. She stumbled back, hitting the bookshelves with a thud. Books tumbled to the floor, their pages rustling like whispers of disapproval, mocking my weakness.

"Shit. I'm sorry." I reached for her, my hand outstretched, desperate to bridge the distance, but she flinched, pushing me away, her eyes, once filled with desire, now cold, hard.

"No one does that to me," she said sharply.

"What? Used to getting your own way, are you?" The words were out before I could stop them, fueled by shame and frustration I couldn't contain. Shame at my inability to shift, to be the dragon she needed, the dragon I wanted to be. Frustration at her probing, her pushing, her insistence on uncovering the very weakness I tried so desperately to hide.

"What are you, some princess or something?" The bitterness, a remnant of Elara's betrayal, a poison I thought I had purged from my system, seeped into my tone, twisting my words and making them sound harsher than I intended.

"I am." The quiet affirmation, the regal steel in her emerald eyes, sent a shiver down my spine. *A princess.* The realization, coupled with the memory of our intimacy, the raw vulnerability we had both exposed, made my head spin.

"And your kingdom…" I couldn't say the words.

Her gaze searched mine, a complex mix of desire and… something else. Disappointment? Pity? The uncertainty twisted in my gut, a knot of apprehension tightening with each passing second.

I saw the conflict raging within her, the war between the passion we'd shared and the harsh reality of my brokenness. She wanted me, desired me, even in my human form. But she was disciplined, controlled, her responsibilities, her duty, a heavy cloak she couldn't shed, unlike the wanton creature I had held in my arms just hours before.

The realization stung a sharp jab of regret. "Why did you come here?" I asked roughly.

"I was drawn here," she stated, her gaze fixed on the scattered books, her voice distant, as if she, too, was retreating into herself, seeking refuge from the painful truth. "A green light. Magic, or something."

"There's no magic here," I lied, the words a self-inflicted wound, a bitter reminder of my own powerlessness.

"You are." Her gaze met mine, a flicker of hope, of desperate belief, in her emerald eyes.

"Not anymore." The words were a choked whisper, a confession I couldn't bring myself to fully articulate. I couldn't change into my dragon form. The chilling emptiness where my dragon once resided, the gaping void in my soul.

"You're a fucking dragon. What are you talking about?" Her voice rose, laced with frustration, with a desperate plea for me to be the savior she so desperately needed.

"I've... changed. I'm more human now." The words were bitter, a self-loathing I couldn't quite suppress. "If you want a dragon, go to the clan that kicked me out." I pushed her away, not physically, but with my words.

"I did," she said quietly. "And they wouldn't help me."

The thought pierced through my self-pity, a spark of something protective igniting within me. Despite my better judgment, despite the years of self-imposed isolation, and despite the fear of failing her, I wanted to help her.

She hesitated, her gaze meeting mine, her emerald eyes shimmering with unshed tears, her vulnerability a raw wound that mirrored my own. "The Gloomlings," she whispered, choked with emotion. "They're creatures of shadow, draining the life from my kingdom. My people are dying. The land is withering. My father, the king... he's powerless to stop it. And my uncle… he's using the Gloom to seize the throne."

Each word was a blow, a hammer against the wall of my self-imposed exile, shattering the illusion of safety I had built around myself. I couldn't hide any longer.

Not from her.

Not from myself.

"And y-you need… my dragon fire?" My words faltered, the realization of my own powerlessness a crushing weight in my chest.

"Yes." The single word, spoken with such quiet desperation, was a plea, a prayer, a demand.

"But I don't have that anymore. I haven't shifted in decades. I told you. I can't." There, I'd said the words out loud, admitting my failure.

"Well, now is your chance. Change. Now." Her tone, though desperate, held a note of command, of unwavering belief, a belief that I couldn't comprehend, couldn't reconcile with my own brokenness.

"I would," I said, my heart aching with the impossible desire to be her savior, to be her dragon. "I would for you… for the woman who walked into my bookstore, into my life, and somehow… claimed my heart in a matter of seconds. But I can't."

"You can." Her steadfast faith and her refusal to

accept my weakness were both inspiring and infuriating.

"I'm telling you I can't change anymore." The words were a sob, a final plea for understanding, for forgiveness.

The sorrow in her eyes, the raw desperation, the crushing weight of her kingdom's fate twisted something inside me, a knot of pain and self-loathing tightening in my chest. I felt like a failure, a fraud, a broken promise. I had nothing to offer her, nothing to offer her dying kingdom.

I was just… Rhysand Page.

A bookseller. A man hiding in the shadows of his past, a dragon without fire, a savior who couldn't save.

Mai

"You can't shift?" Disbelief warred with a rising tide of despair. I searched his amber eyes, desperate for a flicker of the fire I had seen just hours before, the fire that had burned so brightly between us, the fire that had reawakened something within me I thought had long extinguished.

He looked away, and his gaze fixed on the scattered books, their pages whispering secrets I no longer cared to hear. I had found a dragon, a powerful creature of myth, a potential savior for my dying kingdom.

But he was broken.

"I haven't shifted in decades," he'd whispered, the words a death knell, shattering the fragile illusion of hope.

The truth of his words, the finality of his tone, hit me like a physical blow. I had been so focused on finding a dragon, on securing his help, that I hadn't considered this possibility.

I had been a fool.

A naïve, desperate fool.

I had wasted precious time in this realm, time I should have spent preparing for the inevitable, for the final assault that would determine the fate of Aethel. I had to get back. I had to face Erebus, even if it meant facing him alone.

A cold dread coiled in my stomach. *Broken.* Not the magnificent dragon of my dreams but a man trapped in a cage of his own making. My carefully constructed hope crumbled, leaving me raw, exposed. Useless.

A broken dragon couldn't save Aethel.

He couldn't save me.

"But… you're a dragon," I argued, clinging to a desperate sliver of denial. "You… you have to be able to shift." My fingers clenched, my nails digging into my palms, a physical manifestation of the fear threatening to consume me.

He shook his head, his dark hair falling into his

eyes, shielding him from my gaze, from the accusation I knew burned within them. Shame, hot and sharp, twisted in my gut. I had gotten swept up in him, drawn by a promise I knew lingered, and now… now I had nothing to offer but a dying kingdom and a broken heart.

But as I turned to leave, my heart a leaden weight in my chest, my gaze snagged on Rhysand. And then I saw it. Not fire, not the dragon I craved, but a faint emerald light. It pulsed gently, rhythmically, like a heartbeat, a vibrant counterpoint to the Gloom's chilling emptiness, a fragile promise in the dim light of the bookstore. The same mesmerizing hue as the spark that had drawn me to him, shimmering around him like a halo, a ghostly echo of the magic we had shared.

Who is guiding him to me?

My own magic, a kindred spark of emerald, leaped in response, intertwining with the light that surrounded him, a silent conversation between ancient powers. It felt familiar. *Like family.* The realization sent a shiver down my spine, a strange mix of hope and foreboding.

Mother? The thought, unbidden, echoed in my mind, sending a wave of grief and longing through me. Tears pricked at my eyes, but I blinked them back, refusing to succumb to despair. Not yet.

"Mai?" Rhysand's voice, laced with concern, drew me back to the present. His arms wrapped around me, his touch surprisingly gentle, a protective warmth easing the ache in my heart.

"I… I found something," I whispered. "Someone. You. You could help my people. You say you're broken. And yet… there's this light around you. My mother… she's guiding me, even from the afterlife."

"I can't," he repeated. "I'm sorry. I wish I could."

I pulled away, searching his eyes, refusing to believe him. "Will you come back with me?"

"Why?" He stared at me, his amber eyes clouded with doubt, not confusion. "I'm useless to you. I'm not the dragon you need." His tone was rough, laced with a self-loathing that mirrored my own. He turned away, his gaze fixed on the scattered books as if seeking solace in their silent pages.

"You are the dragon I need," I insisted, though my heart ached with the knowledge that he might be right. I stepped closer, my hand resting lightly on his arm, a silent plea for him to believe, to hope, as I did. "You might not be able to shift, not yet, but you have knowledge, power that can still help us."

He flinched at my touch but didn't pull away. "What power, Mai?" he whispered, his voice raw with self-doubt. "I'm broken. I'm a shadow of what I once was. What can I possibly offer you, a princess, a warrior, a woman who deserves a dragon, not... this?"

My gaze fell upon the rosewood shelves, drawn to a faint, ethereal glow emanating from behind a stack of ancient texts. The same light that had led me to him, to this bookstore, to this moment, pulsed with a quiet urgency. "Perhaps this," I murmured, reaching for the source of the light, my fingers trembling with anticipation and fear.

I pulled out a small, intricately carved wooden box. Inside, nestled on a bed of faded velvet, lay a teardrop-shaped crystal pulsing with a warm, golden light.

Rhysand's breath hitched. Recognition flared in his amber eyes. "The Dragon's Tear," he whispered, his voice hushed with awe. "I'd forgotten about it."

"Could it help?" I asked, my voice barely a whisper, my heart pounding with a sudden, desperate hope. I held out the box to him, my hand trembling slightly.

He hesitated, his gaze fixed on the crystal, a flicker of fear warring with a desperate longing in his eyes. This small, unassuming crystal, a relic of ancient dragon magic, might be the key to unlocking his power and saving my kingdom, forging a future neither of us could have imagined. But what if it wasn't enough? What if he was truly broken, beyond repair?

"It might," he said, his voice strained, his fingers brushing against mine as he took the box, the contact sending a shiver of anticipation—and a touch of fear—through me. "But I don't know how."

"Come back with me," I said firmly, the words echoing in the stillness of the bookstore. A vow, a promise, a desperate gamble. "There's a bond between us, Rhysand. Something... *more*. I'll help you become a dragon again, and you will help me save my kingdom. We'll face Erebus together. We'll face the Gloom together."

His amber eyes met mine, a flicker of the fire I craved igniting in their depths. "Mai..." he began. He reached out, his fingers tracing the curve of my cheek, the touch sending a shiver down my spine. "I... I want to help you. I need to help you. But..." He hesitated again, the fear returning, clouding his gaze. "What if I can't? What if I'm not enough?"

"You are enough," I whispered, my fingers intertwining with his, drawing strength from his touch, from the fragile connection that had formed between us so quickly, so unexpectedly. "I will help you find your way."

A slow smile spread across his lips, one that reached his eyes, chasing away the shadows and rekindling the fire I craved. "I hope so. Then I can help you."

Relief flooded through me, a physical ache in my chest, the tension easing from my shoulders. I leaned into him, the scent of woodsmoke and old paper a comforting anchor, a reminder of the fragile sanctuary we had found in each other. Hope, a delicate blossom, unfurled in my heart.

But even as I clung to him, the image of Aethel ravaged and dying flashed before my eyes—the skeletal trees, the poisoned rivers, the acrid stench of decay hanging heavy in the air. The screams of my people, the triumphant sneer of Erebus.

He was waiting.

hysand

The portal shimmered, iridescent, then spat me onto the ravaged earth of Aethel. The stench hit me like a physical blow—a cloying sweetness of decay so potent it made my stomach churn. I stumbled back, one hand instinctively covering my nose, the other reaching for Mai.

Her hand, firm and warm in mine, anchored me in the sudden disorientation. "This…" I breathed, my gaze sweeping over the desolate landscape, the vibrant tapestry in my bookstore a cruel mockery of the reality before me. "This is… Aethel?"

Mai nodded, her emerald eyes shimmering with

unshed tears. Her silence was more eloquent than any words, a palpable sorrow radiating from her, a weight settling on my chest, constricting my breath. It wasn't just grief. It was a sorrow intertwined with magic, with the very essence of this dying land.

I forced myself to breathe, to acclimate to the oppressive atmosphere. The thick air clung to the back of my throat. Beneath that sweetness, another scent—ancient, malevolent—a whisper of shadow and decay that prickled my skin and raised the hairs on my arms. My dormant dragon senses stirred, a low growl rumbling deep within me.

We walked in silence, the only sound the crunch of brittle leaves and dry twigs underfoot. Skeletal trees lined the path, their branches twisted and bare, reaching toward a sky the color of bruised flesh. The earth was blackened, cracked, as if ravaged by fire. No vibrant moss, no wildflowers—only a desolate expanse of decay. A sickly, greenish glow pulsed from the shadows, casting an eerie, unnatural light. This wasn't just a kingdom in decline. It was a world teetering on the brink.

I kept glancing at Mai. Her slender form was tense beside me, her wings now visible, twitching restlessly. She carried the weight of this devastation, the grief of a thousand lost lives etched onto her beautiful face. I had seen sorrow in the human world, but this was different. This was a sorrow woven with magic, with the very fabric of this dying land. It resonated deep within me, awakening a fierce protectiveness I hadn't felt since Elara, an urge to shield Mai from this all-consuming darkness.

We reached a clearing. The air, colder, heavier, the silence broken only by the whisper of wind through dead branches. Mai stopped, her body trembling, her emerald eyes fixed on a scorched patch of earth. She kneeled, her fingers tracing the outline of the blackened soil, her touch reverent.

"She was here," she whispered, her voice thick with unshed tears. "My mother. This is where the Gloom took her." I kneeled beside her. "The first wave," she continued, her voice hollow, distant. "Erebus used the Gloomlings to drain her. They don't leave marks. Just... this..." She gestured at the barren earth, a silent testament to the Gloom's insidious power.

I placed my hand on her back, the warmth of her skin a stark contrast to the coldness in my heart. The Demonology text, heavy in my satchel, suddenly felt like a lifeline. I pulled it out, the worn leather strangely warm. "Perhaps this holds a clue," I said, offering it to her. "A way to fight them, to banish them."

She took the book, our fingers brushing. A spark

of energy, faint but familiar, emerald green like her eyes, arced between us. She opened the text, brows furrowed in concentration, lips moving silently as she scanned the ancient words. I watched her, my heart aching.

The emerald light of her magic, usually so vibrant, was now dimmed, flickering like a dying ember. This world, this Gloom, was draining her too. And in that moment, the desire to help, to protect her, to fight for this ravaged kingdom surged within me, stronger than any fear, stronger than any memory of my own past failures.

I might not be the dragon she needed, not yet. But I was something. And I would find a way to be enough.

CHAPTER 9

Mai

Dread, cold and sharp, twisted in my gut, coiling tighter with each step closer to the castle. The decaying landscape of Aethel, once a familiar ache, now felt like a gaping wound, the stench of death and decay clinging to the air, a suffocating reminder of my failure.

I glanced at Rhysand, his amber eyes scanning the blighted surroundings, a flicker of horror—or was it pity—in their depths. He reached for my hand, his touch hesitant, a silent question. I intertwined our fingers, his warmth a stark contrast to the icy fear that gripped my heart. He had seen the tapestry in his bookstore, the vibrant lie of my kingdom. Now, he was seeing the truth. And I was terrified of what he would see in me—a princess who had promised a savior and returned with a broken man.

The skeletal trees, their branches twisted and gnarled, clawed at the bruised sky, their silence more accusatory than any scream. The earth beneath our feet, blackened and cracked, crumbled like ash, the vibrant moss and wildflowers of my memory replaced by a desolate expanse of decay.

Rhysand's grip tightened on my hand, his breath catching audibly. He hadn't spoken since we left the clearing, his silence a heavy weight in the air, amplifying my own growing sense of dread.

As we approached the castle gates, a figure emerged, his armor gleaming in the fading light. Theron. Relief, sharp and fleeting, warred with the fear that still coiled in my gut. He stiffened as he saw Rhysand beside me, his hand instinctively going to the hilt of his sword, suspicion clouding his normally clear blue eyes. I immediately released Rhysand and stepped forward, trying to create some space.

"Commander," he greeted, his voice tight with unspoken questions. "Were you successful?"

Before I could answer, a booming voice, laced

with a chilling undercurrent of fear, echoed from the battlements. "Mai! Report!"

My father, King Eldrin, his silver hair gleaming in the torchlight, his face etched with worry lines, strode toward us. The weariness in his posture, the way his shoulders slumped beneath the weight of his crown, seemed to have aged him decades. He stopped before us, his gaze sharp, assessing, flickering between Rhysand and me. A gaggle of courtiers, their faces a mixture of morbid curiosity and barely concealed apprehension, hovered in the background, their hushed whispers like the rustling of dead leaves.

"Father," I began, my voice strained. "This is Rhysand. He—"

"One dragon shifter," my father interrupted, his gaze fixed on Rhysand, a flicker of desperate hope warring with suspicion in his eyes. He could sense Rhysand's power, the dormant magic that clung to him, a subtle thrumming in the air, but it was faint, muted, like a dying ember. "Is this the savior you promised, Mai? The one who will wield the dragon fire and banish the Gloom?"

Rhysand stiffened beside me, his jaw tight, his amber eyes flashing with anger and humiliation. I stepped forward, placing my hand on his arm, my touch a silent plea for him to remain calm, my heart pounding a frantic rhythm against the rising tide of despair.

"He is, Father," I said firmly, though my stomach churned with uncertainty. "The journey… it has weakened him. He needs time." The lie, a bitter taste on my tongue, felt like a betrayal, not just to my father, but to myself, to the desperate hope that had driven me to the human realm, the hope that was now crumbling before me like dust.

Before I could continue my desperate charade, Rhysand stepped forward, gently removing my hand from his arm. He held the Dragon's Tear, its smooth surface gleaming in the torchlight, a beacon of false hope. "Your Majesty…" he greeted, his gaze meeting my father's with a steady resolve that surprised me. He closed his eyes, his face pale, his body trembling slightly, as if willing his dragon to emerge. The air crackled with anticipation, the whispers of the courtiers dying down, their gazes fixed on Rhysand, their hopes, their fears, hanging in the balance.

We waited. The silence stretched, taut and agonizing, each second a hammer blow against the fragile shell of my hope. A bead of sweat trickled down Rhysand's forehead, his breathing growing ragged, his body straining with the effort. Still nothing. The Dragon's Tear, clutched tightly in his hand, pulsed with a faint, ethereal light, a cruel mockery of the power it promised, the power he couldn't access.

My father's face hardened, his eyes narrowing, the flicker of hope that had briefly ignited in their depths now extinguished, replaced by a cold, bitter disappointment. "Just as I thought," he said with contempt, his gaze piercing me, sharp as a shard of ice. "There are no dragon shifters who will help us. You've brought back an imposter. A human." He turned away, his tone dripping with disgust, his words a final, devastating blow. "You are no princess of this crown. You blame me for losing battles, but it is you who has failed us. You, with your foolish hopes and empty promises." He strode away, his entourage trailing behind him, their whispers like the rustling of dead leaves, each word a dagger twisting in my gut.

Shame washed over me, hot and suffocating, leaving me exposed, vulnerable, utterly alone. I looked at Rhysand, his face a mask of despair, his shoulders slumped, the Dragon's Tear now a cold weight in his hand. The weight of my kingdom, the lives of my people, and the crushing reality of our impending doom settled upon me, heavier than any crown, heavier than any grief.

What have I done?

CHAPTER 10

hysand

Mai's hand tightened on my arm, her emerald eyes, blazing with anger and defiance, meeting mine. "He's wrong, Rhysand," she said, her voice low, fierce. "You can help us. I know you can." Her unwavering faith, her refusal to accept my weakness were both inspiring and infuriating. I wanted to believe her, to embrace the flicker of hope that ignited within me, but the king's words, sharp as shards of ice, echoed in my mind. *Imposter. Human. Failure.*

"I'm sorry..." I began, the words a choked whisper.

"No," Mai interrupted sharply, her emerald eyes

blazing with a fire that was both fierce and heart-breaking. "I am." Her gaze, filled with a self-directed anger I couldn't comprehend, met mine. "I put you under too much pressure. You told me you hadn't shifted in years. I should have listened." She turned to Theron, her face a mask of cold determination. "Theron, I will meet the troops shortly. Get them ready. I want to see their drills."

She grabbed my hand, her touch surprisingly firm, and pulled me away, down a side corridor, away from the prying eyes and the suffocating weight of expectations. Mai led me to her chambers, the heavy oak door closing behind us with a resounding thud, shutting out the world, the judgment, the despair. I wanted to disappear, to crawl back into the shadows of my bookstore, to pretend this whole nightmare had never happened. *I shouldn't have come,* I thought, the realization a bitter taste in my mouth.

I'm not the hero she needs.

I'm just a broken man.

Mai crossed the room, her movements fluid and graceful, and began to change out of her travel-worn clothes, her back to me, her wings, now visible, shimmering faintly in the dim light. The sight of her, so vulnerable, so strong, sent a conflicting wave of desire and protectiveness through me. I wanted to hold her, to comfort her, to shield her from the pain I had brought into her world. But I knew I couldn't. I had nothing to offer her but empty promises and broken dreams.

She turned, her dark hair now pulled back, her face devoid of makeup, her expression resolute, and my breath caught. She was no longer the seductive creature who had ignited my desire in the bookstore but a warrior, a queen in her own right, her emerald eyes blazing with a fierce determination that both thrilled and terrified me. She donned her armor, each piece a symbol of her strength, her responsibility, and her unwavering commitment to her people. And as she fastened the last buckle, her transformation complete, I felt a different kind of desire stir within me. Not just physical, but a deep, profound admiration for the woman she was.

"I'll be back as soon as I can," she said, her gaze meeting mine, a silent acknowledgment of the unspoken emotions that swirled between us. "There are books in the library. Perhaps you can find something… useful."

I nodded, my throat too tight to speak, and watched as she left, the heavy oak door closing behind her, leaving me alone in the dim light of her chambers, surrounded by the scent of jasmine and woodsmoke, a phantom reminder of the passion we had shared, one that now felt like a cruel mockery of my own powerlessness.

I wandered into the library, the familiar scent of old parchment and decaying leather a strange comfort in this alien world. I picked up a random volume, its pages filled with arcane symbols and forgotten rituals, but my mind was elsewhere, replaying the king's words, Mai's disappointment, and my crushing failure.

I couldn't shift.

I couldn't be her savior.

I was useless.

As I flipped through the ancient text, my gaze snagged on a particular passage. It spoke of the Gloomlings, not as creatures of darkness but as entities summoned from another realm, their forms animated by the stolen life force of Aethel. Puppets dancing on strings of corrupted magic. And then, another passage described a ritual of banishment, a way to sever the connection between the Gloomlings and the summoner, to send them back to the shadowy abyss from whence they came.

My heart quickened, a flicker of hope igniting in my chest. *Banishment...* Perhaps I *could* help. Perhaps I wasn't entirely useless after all. And then, another passage, this one described the destructive properties of dragon fire, how its intense heat could burn through the Gloomlings' stolen energy, releasing the life force they had consumed and restoring it to the land, to the people. A surge of determination coursed through me, stronger than any fear, stronger than any memory of past failures.

I had to shift. I had to find a way.

For Mai.

For Aethel.

For myself.

CHAPTER 11

$\mathcal{M}$ai

We didn't have much time.

I needed a dragon to win this war.

Rhysand was our only hope.

I found him in the library, staring out the window, his amber eyes lost in the swirling shadows gathering beyond the castle walls. He hadn't spoken since the king's dismissal, his silence a heavy weight in the air, a reflection of the shame consuming him. He was a broken hope, perhaps, but our only hope nonetheless.

Time was running out.

I touched his arm, the contact sending a jolt of

emerald fire between us. "Rhysand," I said softly, my voice a gentle caress against the silence. "We have to try again."

He turned and nodded, his amber eyes filled with fear and desperation. His hand found mine, our fingers intertwining, a silent promise passing between us.

"Here?" he asked, his voice barely a whisper.

"The *Codex* spoke of a connection," I murmured, pulling the Dragon's Tear from my pocket, its golden light pulsing faintly in my hand. "A bond that could be strengthened... rekindled... through focused channeling of magic. This place... the library... it's saturated with ancient power. It might be enough."

I placed my hands on his shoulders, my touch sending a shiver through his body. Emerald magic sparked between us, a silent conversation between our souls. I closed my eyes, focusing my will, drawing on the ancient power of the heartwood, the whispers of the ancestors, the raw energy of the earth, channeling it all into him, a conduit of emerald fire, seeking to ignite the dormant dragon within.

My magic, a flickering emerald flame, flowed into him, seeking the dormant fire within, the dragon waiting to be unleashed. His magic, raw and untamed, pushed back against mine, a chaotic dance of fire and shadow, hope and despair. He gasped, his body trembling, muscles coiling beneath my touch. The air crackled with energy, the shadows in the library dancing, twisting. A low growl rumbled in his chest—pain and burgeoning power. For a precious moment, hope soared.

Then, the growl turned into a scream. A raw, guttural cry of pain echoed through the castle walls, tearing at my heart. His body convulsed, skin burning hot beneath my touch. The scent of ozone and burned earth filled the library. The shadows writhed, mirroring his agony. His magic surged and sputtered like a dying flame before collapsing inward, the connection broken. He sagged against me, heavy, lifeless.

The emerald light between us flickered and died. The weight of failure settled upon me, heavy and suffocating. We had failed. Again. Time was running out.

"I'm sorry," he mumbled, staggering as he tried to regain his balance.

The Dragon's Tear was clutched tightly in my hand, its warmth a cruel mockery of the fire we couldn't ignite.

The Nightshade would soon be at our gates.

I had to find another way.

"We'll try tonight," I said, though my stomach

churned. "After the feast. My magic combined with the energy of the ritual, it might be enough to help you shift."

He hesitated, his eyes searching mine, a flicker of doubt in their depths. "Are you sure? Your father—"

"He expects a savior," I interrupted. "I'll give him… a show. For now." I needed that show. I needed the court, the people, to believe that hope remained, even if I wasn't sure I believed it myself. And perhaps, just perhaps, the energy of the crowd, the anticipation, the sheer will of my people, might be the catalyst Rhysand needed, the spark to ignite his dormant dragon fire. "Come," I said, my hand finding his. "We can't keep him waiting."

CHAPTER 12

$\mathcal{M}$ai

The air in the Great Hall crackled with nervous energy, the forced laughter of the courtiers a brittle façade over the fear that permeated the room like the insidious tendrils of Gloom. Torches blazed, casting long, dancing shadows that seemed to mock the false cheer, the hollow celebration.

My father, bless his oblivious heart, had insisted on a feast. A desperate attempt to bolster morale, to project an image of strength and unity in the face of impending doom. He eyed Rhysand, who sat beside me, his eyes reflecting the flickering torches, his jaw tight, his silence a heavy weight in the air. I squeezed

Rhysand's hand, offering an unspoken reassurance I didn't quite feel myself, my smile a strained echo of my father's forced joviality.

The music swelled, a lively, almost frantic melody that did little to mask the underlying tension. My father rose, his goblet held high, his gaze sweeping over the assembled courtiers, lingering for a moment on Rhysand, a flicker of doubt in his eyes. "To Aethel!" he boomed, his voice echoing in the vast hall. "May the ancestors grant us the strength we need to vanquish the Gloom!"

The pointed omission of Rhysand's name, the subtle shift in the toast, hung heavy in the air, a silent acknowledgment of the unspoken tension, the lingering doubt that permeated the room.

The courtiers echoed the toast, their voices strained, their smiles brittle, and I saw the doubt in their eyes. As the ground trembled beneath us, a low, guttural growl echoing through the hall, I knew.

The charade was over.

Chaos erupted. The Gloom. It was here. Two days early. A wave of icy terror washed over me, quickly replaced by a surge of adrenaline, a primal instinct to protect, to defend. The courtiers scattered, their screams a cacophony of terror as the sickly sweet stench of the Gloom filled the air, the taste of it bitter on my tongue.

Rhysand's hand gripped mine, his fingers tightening, his amber eyes wide with alarm. "Mai!" he shouted. "We have to—"

But it was too late. A wave of Gloom, thick and viscous as liquefied night, poured into the hall, its chilling touch extinguishing the torches and plunging us into a suffocating darkness. The screams of my people, their life force being drained away, their magic extinguished, pierced through the darkness, each cry a dagger twisting in my gut. I could feel the Gloom's icy tendrils snaking across the floor, reaching for me, their touch promising oblivion. Rhysand pulled me back, his arm a steel band around my waist, shielding me with his body, his warmth a fragile barrier against the encroaching darkness.

And then, I saw him.

Erebus.

He stood at the entrance to the Great Hall, his face illuminated by the sickly green glow, his eyes burning with triumphant malice.

He raised his hand, and a wave of Gloomlings, their shadowy forms writhing and twisting, surged toward us.

My father, his face pale but resolute, stepped in front of me, his sword drawn, a flickering flame of defiance in the encroaching darkness.

"Run, Mai!" he shouted above the chaos. "Save yourself!"

But I couldn't leave him. I wouldn't. I raised my hands, summoning my own magic, a spark of emerald fire in the suffocating Gloom, but it was too weak, too late. The Gloomlings swarmed over my father, their chilling touch draining his life force, his magic, his very essence. He crumpled to the floor, his sword clattering against the stone, his light extinguished.

"No!" I screamed.

Rhysand pulled me away, his arm a steel band around my waist, dragging me through the chaos, through the screams, through the darkness. We didn't stop running until we reached the relative safety of the hidden library, the heavy oak door slamming shut behind us, a fragile barrier against the horrors that raged outside.

I sank to my knees, the cold stone floor searing my skin through the thin fabric of my gown. My father was gone. Murdered. The weight of the crown, a physical manifestation of my failure, pressed down on me, heavier than any grief. The sounds of battle, of steel clashing against steel, of the Gloomlings' guttural roars echoed through the hidden passage that led to the library, a constant reminder of the war raging just beyond the stone walls, of the lives hanging in the balance.

I looked at Rhysand, his face etched with sorrow, his amber eyes reflecting the flickering candlelight, and a fresh wave of guilt, sharp and bitter, washed over me. I had brought him here, to this dying kingdom, to share in my despair. *And he couldn't even...* I pushed the thought away, the raw disappointment a painful knot in my gut. I had to be strong. For my people. For Aethel.

Suddenly, the heavy oak door burst open with Theron staggering in, his armor battered, his face grim, his sword dripping with the sickly green residue of the Gloom. He slammed the door shut behind him, the sound echoing in the sudden silence of the library, a fragile barrier against the chaos that raged outside.

His gaze swept over the room, taking in the huddled figures of the courtiers, their faces pale with fear, their eyes wide with disbelief. Then, his eyes met mine, and he kneeled, not with the crown, but with my father's sword, its hilt worn smooth with age, its blade still stained with the residue of the Gloom. He offered it to me, not as a symbol of my ascension, but as a weapon, a call to arms.

"All hail Queen Mai!" Theron's voice, strong and

steady, cut through the silence in the library where we hid with others who had fled the surprise attack.

My gut roiled, the taste of bile rising in my throat. The sounds of battle echoed closer, the clash of steel, the guttural roars of the Gloomlings, and the screams of the dying seeping through the thick stone walls of the library, a chilling reminder of the carnage unfolding just beyond our sanctuary.

I looked at the faces of my court, so few remaining, their eyes reflecting the flickering candlelight, the shadows of fear and doubt deepening with each echoing roar, each desperate cry. No. I would not let them succumb to despair. Not while I still drew breath. Not while the fire of defiance, however faint, still flickered within me.

"My father, King Eldrin, died protecting his people," I shouted, my voice ringing with a newfound strength, a fierce determination that surprised even myself. "He died fighting for Aethel. And I swear to you, on his memory, on the sacred blood of our ancestors, that I will not let his sacrifice be in vain! We will not yield to the Gloom! We will not bow to Erebus! We will fight! We will reclaim our kingdom! And we will avenge our fallen!"

A murmur spread through the court, a spark of hope igniting in their eyes. I gave swift, decisive orders. "Theron, take a squad and secure the Great Hall. Prepare for the next attack. The rest of you, with me!"

My hand tightened on my father's sword, the cold steel a comforting weight. With Rhysand and Theron at my side, we pushed open the library doors and stepped into the dimly lit corridor. The sounds of battle echoed from the Great Hall, the clash of steel against steel, the guttural roars of Gloomlings, a chilling symphony of chaos. We advanced, our footsteps echoing on the stone floor, the air thick with the stench of the Gloom, a cloying sweetness mingled with the metallic tang of blood.

As we burst into the Great Hall, a wave of emerald fire erupted from my fingertips, incinerating the Gloomlings that swarmed near the entrance, their shadowy forms dissolving into nothingness with shrieks of despair. Theron and Rhysand, their swords a blur of motion, engaged the remaining Nightshade warriors, their movements swift and deadly. I pressed forward, my own blade singing through the air, each strike fueled by my grief, my rage, my unwavering determination to avenge my father.

With a final, desperate surge of magic, I unleashed a wave of pure emerald energy, banishing the remaining Gloom from the hall, the sickly green glow receding like a tide, leaving behind the flickering light of the torches and the scattered bodies of the fallen.

The effort left me weak, my magic depleted, and a tremor running through my limbs. I leaned against a nearby pillar, my breath coming in ragged gasps, the world tilting precariously around me. The victory, small and fleeting, was a pyrrhic one. I had banished the Gloom from the Great Hall, but at a cost. My magic was almost gone, and the war… the war had just begun.

My gaze fell on Rhysand, his face grim, his amber eyes filled with admiration and concern. *If only he could shift.* The thought was a painful reminder of our dwindling options. But I wouldn't give up. Not on him. Not on Aethel. I would find a way.

Even if it meant sacrificing everything.

"Theron," I said. "Get everyone ready, move anyone from the library who can't fight to the catacombs and lock them in."

He hesitated, his gaze searching mine, a flicker of doubt in his eyes. "As you wish, Your Majesty."

"Then get the soldiers assembled. We will face the Gloom now." My voice rang with a newfound authority, my gaze sweeping over my warriors, igniting a spark of hope in their weary eyes. "Send out the scouts, find out where my uncle is. I want him dead."

I sounded like my father. But without a dragon to help us fight, all we could do was stand together and hope for a miracle.

CHAPTER 13

 hysand

"Mai, I have a better idea." I stepped closer, my hand reaching out to touch her arm, a silent plea for connection, understanding. But she flinched away, her touch, once so warm and welcoming, now a chilling reminder of the chasm that separated us, the dragon fire I couldn't provide. The rejection felt like a physical blow, as if she'd ripped my heart out with the gesture.

"You are of no use," she said, her tone cold, hard, her emerald eyes blazing with grief, anger, and a chillingly familiar despair. "I should've sent you down to the catacombs with the wounded."

Her words, sharp edges of ice, ripped through me, but I held my ground, my own desperation, my own need to help, stronger than any fear of rejection. "I can still help," I insisted. "I might not have my dragon fire, but I have… other weapons."

"Like what?" She turned away, her back to me, her wings heavy and useless, drooping behind her like a fallen angel. "Your wit? Your charming smile? Those won't stop the Gloomlings, Rhysand. They won't save Aethel."

"Your uncle is likely hiding behind the defense of the Gloom, but also his armies," I said. I gained confidence as I laid out my plan, my mind racing, searching for a solution, a way to prove my worth. "He doesn't want to risk being killed. He'll be surrounded by his most powerful warriors, his Gloom-wielding mages. A direct assault would be suicide."

"That's obvious," she retorted.

"So, why don't we use that to our advantage?" I pressed. "We'll circle around to the east, using the hidden passage. Theron can provide a diversionary attack at the main gate and draw Erebus' forces, leaving the eastern flank vulnerable. We'll strike at his command tent, take him by surprise. A small, swift strike force led by you and me. We can end this war… tonight."

"Because the Gloom is everywhere," she snapped, turning to face me, her eyes flashing with anger. "They will suck us dry before we get within a mile of the stronghold."

"No," I countered, my gaze holding hers. "He will have concentrated his forces at the front. He thinks he has won with this surprise attack. He knows the king is dead. He'll be overconfident. Careless."

"It's too risky," she said, shaking her head. "He would kill us before we even got close."

"There's another way," I said, my mind racing, the memory of a passage from the Demonology text, a hidden detail I had almost overlooked, surfacing in my mind. "A hidden passage. Used for… less savory exchanges, I imagine. It should be on the eastern side of the castle, concealed by a cluster of shadow willows."

"How do you know this?" she asked, swinging the sword in a series of practiced movements, the blade whistling through the air, a deadly dance of grief and rage. I couldn't imagine what she was feeling, the weight of her father's death, the responsibility of leading her people in this desperate war, all while battling her own personal demons. And I, the broken dragon, the savior who couldn't save, had only added to her burden.

"I saw it in one of the books in your library," I

said. "This is our best chance of getting past their main defenses. Erebus will expect a direct assault. He won't be expecting us to…"

My words were cut short by the arrival of a scout, his dark armor stained with mud and the telltale greenish residue of the Gloom, his face pale with exhaustion. He bowed his head before Mai. "Your Majesty," he said. "I've located a hidden passage on the eastern side of the castle, concealed by a stand of shadow willows. It appears to lead directly out of the grounds, toward the eastern forest."

Mai's gaze met mine, her emerald eyes widening slightly, a flicker of surprise, and was that a touch of respect in their depths? "Good work," she said to the scout. Then, she turned to me, her expression unreadable, her hand reaching to a nearby body, picking up the sword from the ground. Its hilt worn smooth with age, its blade gleaming faintly in the dim light, and offered it to me, hilt first. "You'll need this," she said, her gaze holding mine, a silent acknowledgment of my determination, my willingness to fight beside her, even in my human form.

I took it, its weight surprisingly comforting in my hand, the cold steel a tangible reminder of the danger we faced, the responsibility I now carried. "Thank you," I murmured, my heart pounding with gratitude and a renewed sense of purpose. I might not be the dragon she needed, not yet. But I would fight.

For her.

For Aethel.

For the fragile hope that had taken root within me, a hope that whispered, perhaps, I could still be enough.

"Let's go," she said sharply, her gaze fixed on the distant fortress, a warrior queen leading her people into battle. I followed, my hand gripping the hilt of my borrowed sword, ready to face whatever awaited us in the shadows.

But before she slipped past my reach, I turned her, pulling her to me with a fierce need to claim her. She released a gasp of shock and confusion pulled at her pinched expression. There was no time for words, and when she opened her mouth, no doubt to question me, I slammed my lips to hers.

Mai tensed, but in the next breath, she wrapped her arms around me, her tongue battling mine for control. I groaned. I couldn't help it. My arousal, no doubt, pressed against her as I slipped a hand around her waist.

Knowing time was of the essence, I reluctantly let her go and stepped back. She was panting for breath and again, when she started to speak, I cut her off. "Go. I'm right behind you."

With that, she dipped her chin and turned, and as promised, I was hot on her heels.

The hidden passage was narrow and damp, the air thick with the scent of mildew and decay, the silence broken only by the soft drip of water and the echo of our footsteps on the damp stone floor. The darkness was absolute. The only light was that of the faint, ethereal glow of Mai's magic, a comforting presence in the suffocating blackness.

We moved quickly, silently, our senses heightened, our bodies tense. Every rustle, every shadow, a potential threat. I could feel Mai's magic, a vibrant emerald current, flowing beside me, a silent reassurance in this oppressive darkness.

The passage opened abruptly into the eastern forest, the night air cool and crisp, a welcome relief. The sickly green glow of the Gloom, though still present, was less intense, diluted by the starlight that filtered through the canopy. We moved swiftly through the trees, following Mai's lead. Her movements were fluid, graceful, her senses attuned to the subtle shifts in the forest, the whispers of magic in the air. She was a creature of this world, of this darkness, and I, the outsider, followed, trusting her instincts, her knowledge, her strength.

We continued moving through the dense undergrowth, the sounds of battle growing louder with each step. The clash of steel, the guttural roars of Gloomlings, the shouts of the Dark Fae—a chaotic symphony of war drawing ever closer. Mai paused, her hand raised, signaling us to halt. We crouched in the shadows of a towering oak, its branches heavy with moss, its roots gnarled and ancient. From our vantage point, we could see the Nightshade fortress, its dark towers silhouetted against the bruised sky, the sickly green glow of the Gloom pulsing around its walls like a malignant heartbeat. Below, the Nightshade forces, their shadowy forms illuminated by the eerie light, swarmed the main gates, their attention focused on the diversionary attack Theron was leading. They were positioned perfectly, a wave of darkness poised to crash against the fortress walls, leaving their rear flank exposed, vulnerable.

"Now," Mai whispered, her eyes blazing with a fierce determination.

We burst from the forest. Beside me, Mai fought with the grace and ferocity of a predator, her emerald fire blazing, her wings a blur of motion as she cut a path through the Gloomlings, leaving me behind, struggling to keep up.

Panic flared in my chest as I lost sight of her in the swirling chaos of the battle. *Mai!* The name, a silent scream, echoed in my mind. I wielded my sword, a desperate, clumsy dance of defense, wounding a few of the shadow warriors as I pushed forward, searching for her, my heart pounding with a fear that was stronger than any I had ever known.

Then, through a break in the swirling shadows, I saw her. Across the courtyard, locked in a desperate struggle with Erebus. His shadowy form towered over her, his laughter, a chilling counterpoint to the screams of the dying, echoing through the night. Mai fought with a ferocity that belied her size, her emerald fire flickering against the overwhelming darkness of his Gloom, but she was losing. He was toying with her, his movements effortless, his power absolute. My heart lurched in my chest, a painful spasm of fear and helplessness. I have to reach her.

He raised his hand, a wave of pure Gloom surging toward her, promising oblivion. Something within me snapped—the fear, the shame, the years of suppressed rage—it all coalesced into a single, over-whelming need.

Protect her.

A searing agony ripped through me, my bones grinding, reshaping, my skin burning as if engulfed in flames. My wings, powerful and leathery, erupted from my back, tearing through the confines of my human clothes, shredding the last vestiges of my self-imposed prison. A roar, a primal scream of rage and defiance, tore from my throat.

I launched into the sky, my wings powerful and sure, carrying me effortlessly above the carnage, the wind whipping through my scales, a symphony of power and freedom, a song of rebirth. Below me, the Gloomlings swarmed, their shadowy forms a writhing mass of darkness, their guttural roars now a pathetic whimper beneath the thunder of my wings. I inhaled, drawing deep into my lungs the magic of Aethel, the raw, untamed power of this ancient land, the fire of my dragon heart, and then exhaled, unleashing a torrent of blue-white flames, a cleansing fire that incinerated the Gloomlings.

Their screams echoed in the night as they dissolved into nothingness. Erebus, his face contorted in surprise and rage, his triumphant sneer replaced by a mask of pure hatred, turned his gaze toward me, his eyes burning with a fire that mirrored my own.

$\mathcal{M}$ai

The world exploded.

Not just in a blinding flash of bronze and gold but in a symphony of fire and fury, the air rippling with the raw, untamed power of Rhysand's transformation, the very earth trembling beneath the thunder of his roar. I shielded my eyes, my body momentarily paralyzed, not just by the sudden shift in power but by the sheer assault on my senses.

The heat of his fire, a searing wave of pure dragon fury, washed over me, scorching my skin, pushing back the encroaching Gloom, its sickly sweet scent of decay momentarily obliterated by the acrid tang of ozone and burning shadow. The ground vibrated beneath my feet, a frantic drumbeat against the rising tide of hope, the sound of Rhysand's wings, like thunder, echoing in my ears, a deafening roar that drowned out the screams of the dying, the cries of the wounded, the whispers of despair.

Rhysand, a magnificent beast of bronze and gold scales, his eyes blazing with a fire that mirrored the inferno within him, soared above the battlefield, his wings, vast and powerful, eclipsing the poisoned sky, his roar a challenge, a promise of vengeance, a declaration of war to the encroaching darkness.

His fire was a torrent of blue-white flames, a cleansing inferno that tore through the ranks of Gloomlings. Their shadowy forms dissolved into nothingness with shrieks of despair, their stolen life force released in a wave of pure energy that washed over me, tingling against my skin, reawakening my own dormant magic, a symphony of emerald and gold.

The land itself seemed to sigh in relief, the earth beneath my feet softening, the skeletal trees trembling with nascent life, the sickly green glow of the Gloom receding, devoured by Rhysand's flames, replaced by the soft, ethereal glow of the rising moon. Aethel was already healing, the land drawing strength from Rhysand's fire, from the resurgence of my own magic, a rebirth of hope and life in the heart of darkness.

And then, I felt it. Not just a surge of power but a flood, raw and untamed. It flooded back into me, rekindling the emerald fire that had flickered and dimmed under the oppressive weight of the Gloom, now blazing with a renewed intensity, a fierce, exhilarating power that pulsed through my veins, a symphony of freedom and defiance.

My wings snapped open, their emerald light a beacon in the night, a promise of vengeance, a symbol of Aethel's enduring spirit. Hope, fierce and exhilarating, surged through me, a tidal wave washing away the despair, the grief, the fear, leaving behind only the cold, hard certainty of purpose. "I am Mai Nightbloom, Queen of Aethel," I roared, my voice echoing Rhysand's challenge to the darkness. "I will not yield!"

I rose into the air, my wings carrying me effortlessly, a warrior reborn, toward Erebus, who stood frozen, his face contorted in a mask of disbelief and rage, his shadowy form flickering, unstable, dissolving, in the receding Gloom. "You... you fool," he snarled, his tone laced with venom, his eyes burning with a hatred that mirrored my own, a hatred fueled by grief, by loss, by the burning desire for vengeance. "Did you really think a broken dragon could defeat me?"

"He's not broken anymore," I argued. My father's sword was a gleaming extension of my will, singing a song of death in the night. "And neither am I. You murdered my parents, Erebus. You tried to steal my kingdom. You unleashed this darkness upon my people. And now… you pay." The words, cold and hard, were not just a threat but a promise. A vow.

Our battle was a clash of titans, a whirlwind of emerald fire and shadowy Gloom, of ancient magic and raw power. I wielded my father's sword, the blade singing through the air, each strike fueled by my grief, my rage, my unwavering determination to avenge his death. "You thought you could control the Gloom, Erebus," I taunted. "But it's consuming you. It's turning you into the very monster you claim to despise."

Above us, Rhysand, a blazing inferno in the sky above, rained down fire, his roars shaking the very foundations of the fortress, the heat of his flames burning away the Gloom, weakening Erebus, his shadowy form flickering, fading as his power waned.

The torrent of blue-white flames tore through the ranks of Gloomlings. Their stolen life force released in a wave of pure energy that washed over the blighted landscape, a cleansing fire that left behind not ash and shadow, but the sweet scent of rain and the promise of new growth.

"This ends now, Erebus," I said as I lunged forward, my father's sword plunging into his chest, the blade piercing his shadowy heart, a symbolic blow that avenged not just my father but all the lives he had stolen.

Erebus screamed, a sound of pure, unadulterated rage and despair as his form dissolved into shadow, the Gloom that had clung to him, to Aethel, receding, retreating back to the abyss. The land sighed, a collective breath of relief, as the sickly green glow vanished, replaced by the soft light of the rising moon. The stench of decay faded, replaced by the fresh scent of rain and damp earth, the first signs of Aethel's rebirth.

The remaining Nightshade, their leader gone, their power weakened, their hope extinguished, threw down their weapons, their shadowy forms collapsing onto the ground, their eyes wide with fear, their bodies trembling.

For now, the war was over.

But as I stood there amidst the ruins of the fortress, the cheers of my warriors, raw and ragged, echoing in the night, a chilling premonition, a cold knot of unease, tightened in my gut. Rhysand hadn't landed. He was still soaring above, a blazing inferno against the moonlit sky, his roars echoing through the night, now filled with something else.

Something wild.

Something feral.

"Rhysand, come to me!" I commanded, my magic reaching out to him, a beacon in the darkness.

But he didn't listen. He didn't even seem to hear.

"Rhysand!" I cried out again, the cheers of my warriors fading, replaced by a shared unease, their gazes, mirroring my own fear, fixed on the dragon spiraling higher and higher into the moonlit sky.

His roars grew louder, more frantic, more animalistic as if he were battling some unseen enemy, some inner demon. He was a molten streak against the velvet canvas of night, the beat of his wings a frantic tattoo against the silence. The bronze and gold of his scales, once so vibrant, now seemed to flicker and distort in the moonlight as if the very essence of his being was unraveling, consumed by the untamed power of his dragon form. And as I watched him disappear into the swirling clouds, a new fear, sharper, more potent than any I had ever known, a fear that tasted of ash and shadow, took root within me, coiling around my heart, constricting my breath.

What have I unleashed?

CHAPTER 15

*M*ai

The silence in the aftermath of the battle was deafening, broken only by the crackling of dying embers, the distant groans of the wounded, and the frantic beating of my own heart. Rhysand was gone. Vanished. The image of his dragon form, a blazing inferno against the moonlit sky, burned in my mind, a terrifying reminder of the power I had unleashed, a power I now feared I couldn't control.

A cold dread, sharp and insistent, coiled in my gut. "Rhysand," I called out into the stillness of the night, my magic reaching out, searching, yearning for a connection, a sign, anything. *Where are you?*

My wings, heavy with exhaustion, carried me above the ravaged battlefield. The scent filling my nostrils was a grim testament to the devastation, the victory we had bought with blood and sacrifice. The ground below was littered with the shadowy remnants of Gloomlings, their forms dissolving into dust. I searched for him, my gaze scanning the skies, my heart pounding with a fear that was more potent than any I had ever known.

What if he couldn't shift back? What if the dragon had consumed him entirely? The thought was a chilling whisper in the back of my mind.

And then, I saw him. Not the magnificent, fearsome dragon I had witnessed just moments before, but a smaller, more vulnerable form perched atop the highest tower of the Nightshade fortress, his bronze and gold scales dulled, his wings drooping, his head bowed. Relief, so profound it almost buckled my knees, washed over me, quickly followed by a new wave of concern.

Something was wrong.

I landed beside him, my own wings folding behind me, my heart aching at the sight of his exhaustion, his vulnerability. He looked up, his eyes no longer blazing with dragon fire, but the familiar warm amber of his human form was filled with weariness. He shifted, his dragon form shrinking, reshaping, the process slow, agonizing, as if each movement were a Herculean effort. He stumbled, his human form, naked and vulnerable, trembling, his breath coming in ragged gasps.

"Rhysand," I choked out with emotion. "Are you… all right?"

He leaned into my touch, his eyes closing, a shudder running through his body. "I… I don't know," he murmured roughly, strained, a flicker of fear in his amber eyes as he opened them. "It's… different now. The dragon… it feels… hungry. Like a part of me I can't… control. I almost didn't… come back."

I nodded, my heart aching for him, for the burden he now carried, the power he had reclaimed, a power that both thrilled and terrified me. "We'll figure it out," I promised, my gaze holding his, a silent promise, a shared burden.

We returned to Nightspire, the castle now eerily silent, the echoes of battle replaced by the whispers of the wounded, the quiet sobs of those who had lost loved ones, and the scent of blood and smoke clinging to the air.

The people emerged from the catacombs, their faces pale, their eyes filled with fear and hope, their voices hushed, reverent as they looked upon me, their new queen. The weight of their gazes, the weight of their expectations, settled upon me, a heavy cloak of responsibility.

Theron approached, his armor stained with the residue of battle, his face grim, but his eyes held a newfound respect, a glimmer of hope. "Your Majesty," he greeted. "The Nightshade have surrendered. Their forces are scattered, their leader gone. The Gloom has receded. Aethel is safe. For now."

The 'for now' hung in the air, a chilling reminder of our continued vulnerability, the ever-present threat of the Gloom's return. I nodded, the weight of the crown, though still heavy, no longer a burden but a symbol of hope, of resilience, of the enduring spirit of my people.

Soon after the battle and the burial of those lost, my official coronation took place. I vowed to protect my people, to rebuild our kingdom, to honor my father's legacy, to ensure that his sacrifice would not be in vain.

Rhysand had stood beside me, his human form still radiating a faint, residual warmth from his dragon fire, his amber eyes, though weary, fixed on mine, his presence a silent promise, a source of strength.

He had chosen to stay in Aethel, to embrace his dragon heritage, to stand by my side, not as a savior, but as an equal, a partner, a lover.

In the weeks that passed, the scent of smoke still clung to the air, a ghostly reminder of the battle, of my father's sacrifice. But beneath it, a new scent emerged. The sweet fragrance of moonwillow blossoms, a reminder of their connection to the land, to the magic that flowed through its very veins, and a symbol of Aethel's resilience.

I now stood in the heartwood grove, overseeing the planting of new saplings, a small act of defiance against the darkness. Rhysand stood beside me, his arm around my waist, his warmth a comforting presence. He had learned to control his shifts, the wildness within him now a banked ember, a source of strength, not a raging inferno.

I turned to face him, and he smiled, a slow, seductive curve of his lips that sent a familiar warmth spreading through me, one that had nothing to do with dragon fire and everything to do with the love that bloomed between us, a love as resilient as the moonwillow blossoms. A love as fierce as the dragon within him.

"It's beautiful, Mai," he murmured, his gaze sweeping over the newly planted saplings, the fragile symbols of hope against the backdrop of the scarred landscape. "You've brought Aethel back to life."

"Not alone," I said softly, my fingers tracing the lines of his hand, the calluses a testament to his newfound strength, his commitment to our shared future. "We did this. Together."

A messenger arrived, bearing news not of a Nightshade attack but of a delegation seeking an audience, emissaries from the neighboring kingdoms, their eyes drawn to Rhysand, the dragon who had saved Aethel. The dragon who now stood beside me, not as a conqueror but as a protector.

My heart swelled with a quiet pride, a sense of accomplishment that was both exhilarating and humbling.

But the war wasn't over. We had won a battle, a crucial victory against the encroaching darkness. The whispers of dissent still echoed in the shadows. The Nightshade, though weakened, were not entirely eradicated.

Rhysand's hand tightened around me, a silent promise of support, a shared strength. I knew with certainty that defied logic, we would face whatever challenges lay ahead.

And we would prevail.

ABOUT THE AUTHOR

Lilliana Rose weaves enchanting tales of shifters, witches, and the monsters that lurk in the shadows of the unknown. Love ignites amidst the untamed wilderness, where ancient lore and cryptic prophecies whisper secrets of the past. When she's not conjuring thrilling plots, a quiet evening finds her curled up with a cup of tea (or a glass of red wine) and a book featuring a wolf or dragon on the cover. Lilliana brings a unique blend of logic and imagination to her writing, creating stories that will haunt your dreams and keep you spellbound until the very last page.

ACKNOWLEDGMENTS

Thank you to my writing pal Sprinkles who loves to interrupt me with his wet nose and puppy eyes or a dirty ball.

Thanks to my editors Kaylene and Nikki for polishing up the manuscript.

Thank you HelzKat for a wonderful cover.

www.ingramcontent.com/pod-product-compliance
Lightning Source LLC
Chambersburg PA
CBHW051708180726
48283CB00004B/1256